A NOTE TO PARENTS

Disney's First Readers Level 2 books were created for beginning readers who are gaining confidence in their early reading skills.

Compared to Level 1 books, **Level 2** books have slightly smaller type and contain more words to a page. Although sentence structure is still simple, the stories are slightly longer and more complex.

Just as children need training wheels when learning to ride a bicycle, they need the support of a good model when learning to read. Every time your child sees that you enjoy reading, whether alone or with him or her, you provide the encouragement needed to build reading confidence. Here are some helpful hints to use with the **Disney's First Readers Level 2** books:

★ Play or act out each character's words. Change your voice to indicate which character is speaking. As your child becomes comfortable with the printed text, he or she can take a favorite character's part and read those passages.

★ Have your child try reading the story. If your child asks about a word, do not interrupt the flow of reading to make him or her sound it out. Pronounce the word for your child. If, however, he or she begins to sound it out, be gently encouraging—your child is developing phonetic skills!

★ Read aloud. It's still important at this level to read to your child. With your child watching, move a finger smoothly along the text. Do not stop at each word. Change the tone of your voice to indicate punctuation marks, such as questions and exclamations. Your child will begin to notice how print makes sense and makes reading fun.

★ Let your child ask you questions about the story. This helps to develop your child's critical thinking skills. Use the After-Reading Fun activities provided at the end of each book as a fun exercise to further enhance your child's reading skills.

★ Praise all reading efforts warmly and often!

Remember that early-reading experiences that you share with your child can help your child to become a confident and successful reader later on!

— Patricia Koppman
Past President
International Reading Association

First published by Disney Press, New York, New York.
This edition published by Scholastic Inc.,
90 Old Sherman Turnpike, Danbury, Connecticut 06816
by arrangement with Disney Licensed Publishing.

SCHOLASTIC and associated logos are trademarks of Scholastic Inc.

ISBN 0-7172-6525-0

Printed in the U.S.A.

DISNEY'S THE LION KING
SIMBA'S POUNCING LESSON

by Gail Tuchman

Illustrated by Sol Studios

Disney's First Readers — Level 2
A Story from Disney's *The Lion King*

⭐⭐

SCHOLASTIC INC.

New York Toronto London Auckland Sydney
Mexico City New Delhi Hong Kong Buenos Aires

In the jungle
of monkeys and trees,
swinging vines,
and a cooling breeze,
Timon cried, "Yaaa!
Charge, Pumbaa!"

But when they saw Simba,
the two stopped short.
"What are you doing?"
Pumbaa asked with a snort.

"I was trying to pounce,"
sighed the sad, little cub.
"But I don't know how
to catch any grub."

"We'll teach you to pounce,"
Timon pointed out,
as he tiptoed about
on Pumbaa's big snout.

"First, you tiptoe, nice and slow.
Then you pounce. Ready, set, go!"

"OK," said Simba.
"I'll give it a shake.
Watch me pounce
on that big, purple snake."

Simba said to himself,
First, you tiptoe, nice and slow.
Then you pounce. Ready, set, go!

In the jungle
of monkeys and trees,
swinging vines,
and a cooling breeze,
the purple snake hissed.
And poor Simba missed.

"Try this," said Pumbaa,
"to follow that fly.
Pretend you're a spy.
Creep close, then leap high."

"OK," said Simba.
"I'll give it a try.
I'll pounce on that fly,
as easy as pie!"

Simba said to himself,
*To follow that fly,
I'll pretend I'm a spy.
Creep close, then leap high.*

In the jungle
of monkeys and trees,
swinging vines,
and a cooling breeze,
Simba sneezed.
And the fly was pleased.

"Try again, kid,"
Timon called out,
as he jumped about
on Pumbaa's big snout.

"You need a big *bounce*
to give you your pounce."

"It's the bounce
that counts,
when you pounce!"

"OK," said Simba.
"Let me see.
I'll pounce on that bug,
one, two, three!"

Simba said to himself,
*It's the bounce
that counts,
when you pounce!*

In the jungle
of monkeys and trees,
swinging vines,
and a cooling breeze,
Simba's bounce was too slow,
as he watched the bug go.

Tiptoe. Bounce. Spy.
Creep. Leap. Why?
Words spun around in Simba's head.

Then he remembered what
his father had said:
"Stay low to the ground,
and don't make a sound."
So Simba *quietly* practiced
pouncing around.

Pumbaa and Timon
were sniffing around.
Simba was lurking,
not making a sound.

The cub stayed low,
waiting to go . . .

. . . He pounced on the pair
and gave them a scare!

"*Now* I can pounce,"
Simba proudly announced.

In the jungle
of monkeys and trees,
swinging vines,
and a cooling breeze,
Timon cried, "Yaaa!
HOORAY . . . Simba!"

Enhance the reading experience with follow-up questions to help your child develop reading comprehension and increase his/her awareness of words.

Approach this with a sense of play. Make a game of having your child answer the questions. You do not need to ask all the questions at one time. Let these questions be fun discussions rather than a test. If your child doesn't have instant recall, encourage him/her to look back into the book to "research" the answers. You'll be modeling what good readers do and, at the same time, forging a sharing bond with your child.

SIMBA'S POUNCING LESSON

1. Why was Simba sad?

2. What animals were in the trees?

3. What happened when Simba pounced on the snake?

4. How many pouncing lessons did Timon and Pumbaa give Simba?

5. Whose advice on pouncing did Simba follow?

6. Who did Simba finally scare by pouncing on them?

Answers: 1. he didn't know how to pounce. 2. monkeys. 3. the snake hissed and scared Simba. 4. three. 5. Simba followed his father's advice. 6. Timon and Pumbaa.